Rob Scotton

Love, Splat

SCHOLASTIC INC.
New York Toronto London Auckland
Sydney Mexico City New Delhi Hong Kong

Special thanks to Maria.

ISBN: 978-0-545-23253-1

24 23 22 21 20 19   16/0

Printed in the U.S.A.   40

First Scholastic printing, January 2010

For Liz,

—R.S.

Splat stared into the bathroom mirror.
A worried Splat stared back.
His heart drummed and his tummy rumbled.

He straightened his whiskers,
ruffled his fur, and brushed his teeth.
Today he wanted to look just right.
After all, today was Valentine's Day.

Splat had made cards for everyone in his class.
And he also made a special card for a certain cat in his class . . .

Kitten. She had snowy white paws and pea green eyes,
and Splat liked her more than fish sticks and ice cream.

But whenever Kitten saw Splat,

she pulled his ears and poked his belly,

tied his tail and called him smelly.
Then she'd run away.

"Why does she do that?" Splat sighed.
Seymour shook his head.

Splat practiced his smile one last time and left the bathroom.
His family wished him a very good morning.

He ignored his breakfast and
gazed at a little red envelope.

On the front of the envelope,
in Splat's very best writing,
was a single name . . .

kitten

Splat tucked the envelope in his bag and left for school.
His tummy rumbled loudly all the way.
He was so busy telling his tummy to be quiet that he
didn't see Kitten coming around the corner.

SPLAT!

He bumped into her.

And when he tried to say sorry, his tongue
turned to jelly, his legs wobbled like rubber,

and his tummy rumbled louder than ever.
This happened every time he saw Kitten.

Kitten gave Splat a funny look.
Then she pulled his ears and poked his belly,

tied his tail and called him smelly . . .
                              and ran away.

"Why does she do that?" he sighed.
Seymour shook his head.

Later, in Cat School,
all the class swapped their valentines.

Splat sat at his desk clutching the little red envelope.
"I'll give it to her soon," he said to Seymour.
But soon it was recess.

Splat sat quietly on a bench still clutching the little red envelope.

He didn't see the cat sneaking up behind him.

"Boo!" cried Spike.

Splat jumped . . . and dropped the little red envelope.

Spike picked it up and read the name on the front.

"I like Kitten too," Spike announced.
"And I like her more than you do."

"But I like Kitten this much,"

said Splat.

"And I like her this much,"

said Spike.

"Aww,"

groaned Splat.

Splat pulled a piece of chalk
from his pocket and drew a
heart on the ground.

"I like Kitten this much," he said.

"And I like Kitten this much," said Spike.
And he drew a heart around the whole playground.

"Aww,"
groaned Splat.

"I made Kitten a special valentine card," Splat said.

"You call that a card?" Spike said smugly.

kitten

"Awwww,"

groaned Splat. "It's not fair."

Seymour shook his head.

Splat's card looked teeny-weeny next to Spike's,
and with a sigh, he threw it in the trash.

Kitten opened Spike's card.
The message inside read,
"You are so lucky that I like you."

Kitten smiled.
Splat didn't.

And he turned away.

Splat didn't see the snowy white paws
lift the little red envelope from the trash

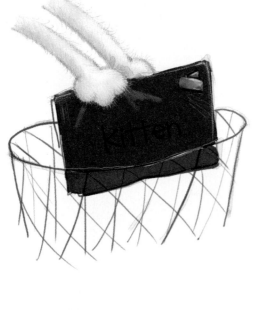

or the pea green eyes read
the name on the front.

Kitten took the card from the
envelope and opened it.

In Splat's very best writing were three little words:

Kitten sat down
next to Splat

and gave him a
little pink envelope.

On the front was a
single name: Splat.
Splat opened the envelope.

And on the card was a rhyme.

Your fur is soft
and I like to stroke it.
You make a silly noise in your belly
when I poke it.
Your tail's so bendy
it makes me laugh,
and you smell really nice
when you've just had a bath.

X

Inside the card, in Kitten's very best writing, were three little words: